Big Cats

and

Duck in the Mud

By Caroline Walker

Illustrated by
Amanda Erb

The Letter C

Trace the lower and upper case letter with a finger. Sound out the letter.

Around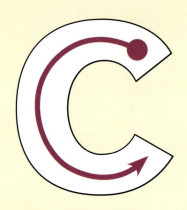

Around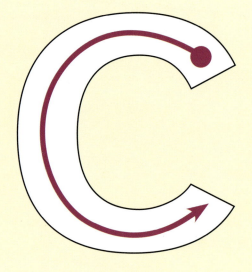

Some words to familiarise:

kitten   cat   tiger

High-frequency words:

is   a   as

Tips for Reading 'Big Cats'

- Practise the words listed above before reading the story.

- If the reader struggles with any of the other words, ask them to look for sounds they know in the word. Encourage them to sound out the words and help them read the words if necessary.

- After reading the story, ask the reader what the biggest cat was.

Fun Activity

Can you name any other big cats, like lions?

Big Cats

Big Cats

and

Duck in the Mud

'Big Cats' and 'Duck in the Mud'
An original concept by Caroline Walker
© Caroline Walker 2023

Illustrated by Amanda Erb

Published by MAVERICK ARTS PUBLISHING LTD
Studio 11, City Business Centre, 6 Brighton Road,
Horsham, West Sussex, RH13 5BB
© Maverick Arts Publishing Limited August 2023
+44 (0)1403 256941

A CIP catalogue record for this book is available at the British Library.

ISBN 978-1-84886-973-8

www.maverickbooks.co.uk

This book is rated as: Pink Band (Guided Reading)
It follows the requirements for Phase 2 phonics.
Most words are decodable, and any non-decodable words are familiar,
supported by the context and/or represented in the artwork.

Sid is a big kitten.

But Sid is not as big as Meg.

Tom is a big cat.

But not as big as a tiger!

A tiger is a big, big cat!

The Letter K

Trace the lower and upper case letter with a finger. Sound out the letter.

*Down,
lift,
down,
down*

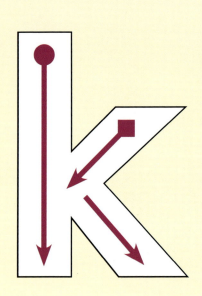

*Down,
lift,
down,
down*

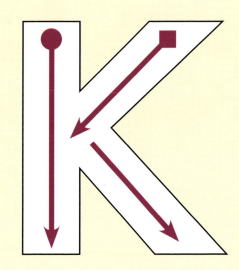

Some words to familiarise:

red   duck   mud

High-frequency words:

a   the   go   of   is   in   it

Tips for Reading 'Duck in the Mud'

- Practise the words listed above before reading the story.

- If the reader struggles with any of the other words, ask them to look for sounds they know in the word. Encourage them to sound out the words and help them read the words if necessary.

- After reading the story, ask the reader which duck won the race.

Fun Activity

Draw a picture of a duck you would enter in a race!

Duck in the Mud

21

Will the red duck win?

The red duck is in the mud!

The big duck pecks it!

Book Bands for Guided Reading

The Institute of Education book banding system is a scale of colours that reflects the various levels of reading difficulty. The bands are assigned by taking into account the content, the language style, the layout and phonics. Word, phrase and sentence level work is also taken into consideration.

Maverick Early Readers are a bright, attractive range of books covering the pink to white bands. All of these books have been book banded for guided reading to the industry standard and edited by a leading educational consultant.

Pink
Red
Yellow
Blue
Green
Orange
Turquoise
Purple
Gold
White

To view the whole Maverick Readers scheme, visit our website at www.maverickearlyreaders.com

Or scan the QR code above to view our scheme instantly!